THE TALE OF

GEALDORS AND RUNES

BOOK 2 OF THE ELLA TRILOGY

CATARINA HANSSON

AuthorHouse™ UK
1663 Liberty Drive
Bloomington, IN 47403 USA
www.authorhouse.co.uk
UK TFN: 0800 0148641 (Toll Free inside the UK)
UK Local: 02036 956322 (+44 20 3695 6322 from outside the UK)

This book is printed on acid-free paper.

ISBN: 979-8-8230-8264-8 (sc)
ISBN: 979-8-8230-8263-1 (e)

Print information available on the last page.

Published by AuthorHouse 06/20/2023

authorHOUSE®

Also by Catarina Hansson

The Tale of Oknytt and Gray Gnomes

The Tale of Dragons and Flatfeet

In Swedish

Tigerspår

Several teachings aids

To my grandchildren

Contents

To begin again ...

Welcome back to Nordanland, where a girl called Tora lives with dwarfs, giants, humans, and elves. But there live also bad people and creatures like the oknytt and the gray gnomes. Have you ever seen a gray gnome or an oknytt? No, they're not very common here, but there are a lot of them living in Nordanland.

Oknytt are rather short creatures with long, floppy ears. They have small, black eyes and yellowish skin. As soon as anyone approaches, human or animal, they become virtually invisible—the oknytt can blend into their surroundings for brief moments, and this ability makes them excellent thieves and spies. Oknytt are vicious but fortunately quite gullible.

The gray gnomes are also quite short, but muscular and strong. They each have a very large nose with which they can track down most things. That's why they often work on finding things and sometimes even people.

I thought I'd tell you about an animal that you may not have seen before, the glutton hog. It is without doubt the biggest wild boar I have ever seen. A glutton hog is huge, of a blackish-grey colour with black eyes and covered in prickly hair. Quite grumpy rascals! So you must be a bit careful when talking to a glutton hog. It might be good to know if you come across one.

We can't talk about who lives in Nordanland without mentioning Tora, who is the main character of this book. Tora is a young girl who is a seid. A seid can see into the future and help the sick. But is that all she is? One day everything changed for Tora. What will happen now? I'm not going to reveal that to you here, but for now you can read about Tora's adventures in peace and quiet.

Names in the Ella Trilogy

Atte	a Black Elf
Birk	an evil sorcerer who is not allowed to live in Nordanland
Botvid	a gray gnome
Brage	an evil, not-so-good magician who works for Jarl Olav
Nidhugg	dragon
Egil	a king of the dwarfs who rules in Nifelheim
Ella	Tora's mother, a strong seid who was queen of Nordanland before her death
Grim	dwarf
Ash, Soot, Black	three ravens
Jarl Olav	the self-proclaimed king of Nordanland, who is stingy and mean
Grandmother	a seid, deceased mother of Queen Ella and grandmother of Tora
Odd	a giant of the Rimtursar family
Odin	the most powerful god in the Aesir faith
Sigrid	a powerful seid who is leader and chief of Fala village, and sister of Tora's grandmother
Solve	Tora's late father, who was king of Nordanland
Thor	god of thunder and weather in the Aesir faith
Tora	a seid and healer, daughter of King Solve and Queen Ella of Nordanland
Trolgar	leader of a gang of gray gnomes
Truls	a magician and healer in the town of North Island
Wolf	Tora's companion wolf
Wolfpelt	leader of the oknytt
Viva	sister of Tora's grandmother, a seid and magician

Notes on the Aesir Faith

Odin is the leader of the Asgardians. He is the god of warriors, can see everything that happens, and is very wise. Odin has two ravens, Hugin and Munin, and the horse Sleipner, which has eight legs. Valhalla is Odin's castle where he receives Vikings who have died in battle.

Thor is, among other things, the god of thunder and the protector of mankind. He is strong and rides across the sky in a chariot pulled by goats. Thor's hammer is called Mjölner.

ELLA'S FAMILY

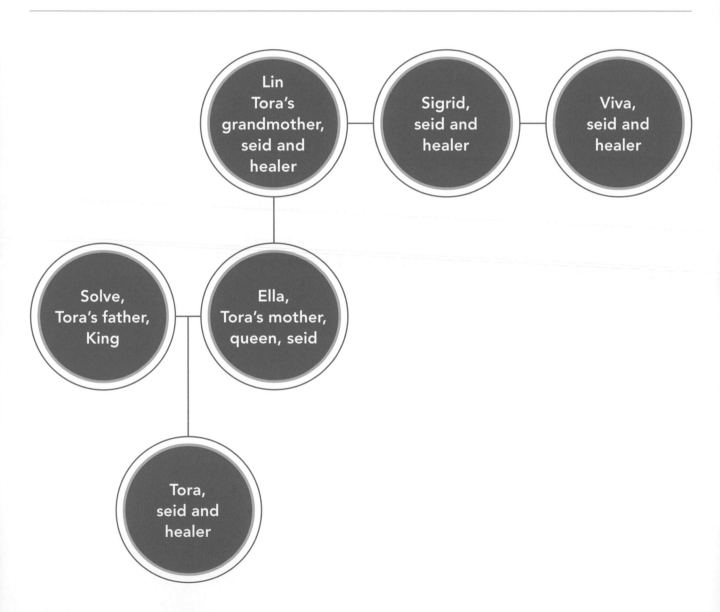

Lin
Tora's grandmother, seid and healer

Sigrid, seid and healer

Viva, seid and healer

Solve, Tora's father, King

Ella, Tora's mother, queen, seid

Tora, seid and healer

What happened in The Tale of Oknytt and Gray Gnomes

Tora is an orphan girl who has lived with her grandmother for about eight years. One day, the villagers came for her grandmother because she was accused of being a witch. Tora then leaves the village and goes into the forest. There she finally gets help from her grandmother's sister Sigrid. Tora, her grandmother, and Sigrid are all strong seids and healers. They can do things such as see into the future, dream true dreams, cure diseases, and talk to animals. Sigrid's other sister, Viva, is a strong, blind magician who lives alone in a cottage in the woods. Viva tries to teach Tora everything she can.

Jarl Olav has made himself king of Nordanland. He kidnaps Tora and burns down Fala village where Sigrid is the leader. The people of the village flee to the dwarfs' cave Nifelheim and gather a large army to free Tora. Tora tricks Jarl Olav and his magician Brage and manages to escape from the castle in the town of Silje to Viva's cottage in the forest. There she stays for the summer with her best friend, Wolf.

Tora is given an enchanted ellacross by Sigrid and Viva for protection. The spell attached to the cross makes it smell bad when an evil person comes near Tora. A long time ago, the god Odin gave several ellacrosses to the seids to use for good deeds. Now both Jarl Olav and the gray gnomes are very keen to have ellacrosses so that they can become rich and powerful.

Time stands still in Viva's cottage, and Tora suddenly discovers that autumn has come to the Ancient Forest. Viva says that a blood moon is approaching and warns that evil forces may grow stronger. Just then there is a knock on the door of the cottage and an elderly, hunched-over man with a long, white beard enters. A faint foul smell spreads through the cottage and they realize they are visited by a dangerous man. Tora and Wolf immediately leave the cottage while Viva offers the mysterious man tea.

1

TORA AND WOLF

Tora and her friend, Wolf, make their way quickly along the path as the Ancient Forest grows darker. They can't see the branches moving and the oknytt, who are looking for them, coming up behind them on the path. Then the oknytt quickly disappear in the other direction, towards the den of the oknytt's leader, Wolfpelt, in the woods.

Tora and Wolf are going to the dwarfs' great cave village of Nifelheim. There lives Sigrid, the leader of all the seids in Nordanland, while her village is being rebuilt after the great fire. Tora and Wolf had to leave Viva's cottage in a hurry when a stranger suddenly appeared.

"Do you know who the old man is?" Tora asks Wolf. "Do you recognize him?"

"No, I don't know who it is," says Wolf. He stops on the path to wonder. "But did it start to smell bad around him, or was it just my sensitive nose?"

"You're right. It started stinking as soon as he walked through the door. The ellacross with its magic still works. The evil ones are starting to smell bad around me. But what does he want?" Tora sighs and scratches her nose thoughtfully.

Then they hear a distant howl through the darkness of the forest. Wolf pricks up his ears and listens, and then tilts his head back and answers so loud it almost hurts Tora's ears. Wolf looks at her and asks, "Can you get to Nifelheim on your own? It's only a short distance away."

"Sure," says Tora, "but what's going on?"

"My friends asked me to come to Viva's cottage. They have something to show me. I'll be back soon. Go straight away without stopping!" Wolf looks at her sternly.

"I'll be fine," laughs Tora. "You run!"

"I can keep you company for a while on the road," says a voice heard from behind a fern on the side of the path. "You go, Wolf, and I'll make sure Little Miss gets to the dwarfs' cave village." There is a rustle as the big leaves of the fern are folded away and a big badger appears on the path. Grey around the nose and squinting, the old badger looks kindly at Tora.

"Shall we leave immediately, perhaps? You never know what nasty things will creep up under cover of darkness."

"Good evening, Mr Badger," says Tora. She gives the old fellow a little nod.

Wolf listens anxiously and then runs towards Viva's cottage, while Tora and Mr Badger start walking towards Nifelheim.

It is getting darker and more difficult to see the path. Badgers are usually awake at night, but Tora is having trouble seeing where she is going.

"Oh, how stupid of me," says Mr Badger as Tora stumbles. "I can see better than you in the dark. One moment, and we'll see if we have any friendly fireflies among the bushes."

The badger pokes his head into the thicket next to the path, and Tora hears him grunt a little. Then the head comes out again, and with it come fireflies.

"So, they have promised to light the path for you all the way to Nifelheim," says Mr Badger, looking pleased. The fireflies light up the path for Tora, and they can walk a little faster.

Beside the path the come upon a very big stone.

"I remember when this stone landed here," Mr Badger says. "It was a sunny day in the summer, and there were flowers everywhere. A troll was walking to the market carrying a lot of stones. Trolls love to sell stuff, you see. The troll picks some flowers and puts his big nose in the bouquet and takes a good sniff. Then, of course, the troll sneezes and drops all the stones. Well, no one got hurt, but the troll didn't pick up this stone. It is a nice stone, though."

Mr. Badger has been alive for many years and can tell stories about almost every stone and tree they pass. Not that Tora believes every story he tells, but it's nice to have company in the night.

After a long walk, the fireflies suddenly start to blink. "We seem to have arrived at Nifelheim," says the badger. "Thank you, fireflies!"

The fireflies go out and disappear into the darkness. Behind the tree trunks, Tora sees light from torches and fires at the dwarfs' great cave village. She has arrived safely.

"Thank you very much," she says to Mr Badger. "It was nice to have company while travelling in the dark."

"Thank you," the badger replies. "It's always nice to have someone to talk to. Good evening!" There is a rustle in the bushes, and the badger is gone.

Tora walks out onto the grass in front of the caves. There dwarfs and elves sit by the fires and talk. People are walking around with food, and there is laughter and chatter everywhere. Tora sighs with relief. She is safe.

"Hello, Tora," a dwarf who has quietly slid up beside greets her. "Welcome! Sigrid is sitting with Egil the Dwarf King in the great hall. You go right in."

"Thank you," Tora replies. She walks towards the largest cave opening.

She enters a room so beautiful that she must stop and look around, and so big that it almost feels like being in a castle. Torches hang around the walls of the huge hall, and the smoke from them smells like lavender. The glow from the torches shines among beautiful, twisting branches of gold that adorn the walls. Large gold candlesticks with silvery candles stand on the long tables made of dark wood. The room fills with the murmur of everyone sitting at the tables.

"Tora, what are you doing here?" Sigrid says. She stands up and waves to the girl as she looks at her with a worried expression. "Where is Wolf? And Viva?"

Nifelheim

Tora makes her way through the people in the great cave hall. She reaches Sigrid and receives a warm hug. Tora hasn't realized how much she has missed Sigrid until now, when she stands there in front of her with her hair a bit dishevelled and a warm smile. But Sigrid looks at Tora worriedly in the light of the torches.

"Well, my friend. Now tell us! What are you doing here so late at night? We were just about to go to bed," says Sigrid. She pulls out a chair for Tora. "Are you hungry? I think there are stomped mush and glutton sausage left."

"Yes, very hungry," says Tora, as she sits down with a sigh.

Only now does she feel how tired and thirsty she is. Mr Badger told her so many stories as they walked through the forest that she forgot she hadn't eaten. *Cunning old fellow*, Tora thinks, smiling. Within a minute there is food and cold water on the table, and she starts to eat immediately.

Word of Tora's arrival in Nifelheim begins to spread, and soon a sleepy Grim Dwarf appears beside the table. He pulls out a chair and sits down, taking a large mug from the table and pouring mead. He drinks almost the entire mug of mead in one gulp, burps loudly, and then leans contentedly against the table. He says, "Hi, Tora!" His face breaks into a big smile, and he laughs so hard that his beard jumps on his slightly too-round belly. "What a pleasant surprise!"

"Hi, Grim!" says Tora with a smile. The friendly dwarf always spreads peace and joy wherever he goes. "I can tell you a little about Niefelheim while you eat, if you like."

Tora nods as she eats the delicious food. "Long ago dragons lived in these caves. The dragons amassed gold and silver and lived like kings here. But they didn't want to clean the caves and fix food, so they hired dwarfs to look after them. One day a large army of people came to Nordanland. They took over the land and chased away the dragons because they were afraid of them. But the dwarfs were allowed to stay in these caves. The humans didn't know there were lots of gold in the caves, so the dwarfs took over all the dragon gold. Now you know why dwarfs are so rich and why dwarfs live in these caves."

"Wow! The humans must have been angry when they realized that the dwarfs got all the gold." Tora smiles and then tells them about the summer with Viva, ending with the strange old man who came unexpectedly to the cottage.

"Are you sure the stench came from the ellacross?" Sigrid asks with worry.

"Yes, unfortunately," Tora replies. "Viva immediately took my bag and told me to leave. I thought it best to do as she said, although I don't really understand why. Wolf called to his friends, but something happened because he had to run back. I'm a bit concerned."

"Yes, we'd better check it out," says Grim, pulling his beard thoughtfully. "Tell me, Sigrid, do you know any foxes nearly who might run off and see what's going on at the cottage?"

"I'll go see who's out there." Sigrid gets up and walks quickly out of the cave.

"You, young lady, are going to bed before you fall asleep at this table," Grim says with a laugh. Tora realizes how sleepy she has become after all the food she's eaten and the heat inside the cave. They get up, and she follows Grim out of the hall to a small room with two beds and a table. Tora sits down on a bed with a deep sigh. She pulls the soft, dark-green blanket over her and falls asleep before Grim has closed the door.

Sigrid asks the foxes Red and Rusty, along with Runar Rat, to run to Viva's cottage deep in the Ancient Forest. They will try to find out what is going on and see if Wolf and his friends need help. Sigrid talks to the dwarfs' guard chief Lita and explains what has happened. Lita promises to gather some volunteer dwarfs and send them to the cottage as soon as the day dawns. Sigrid feels a little calmer now but settles down to sleep in a chair in front of the fireplace in the great hall so she can get the news as quickly as possible when the animals return.

In the meantime, Wolf has reached the cottage in the clearing deep in the Ancient Forest. He sees some of his friends guarding the cottage. He runs up to them and greets them cheerfully, for it has been a long time since they saw each other.

"Is everything okay?" Wolf asks.

"Too calm," replies one of the wolves. "Viva is in her bed, but we can't wake her up. There is a strange smell inside the cottage. It doesn't go away even though we have opened the door and the windows."

"In addition, the fire in the stove has gone out and the lights are off. They cannot be relit. There are an unusually large number of spiders in the cottage, or so we think. You never know with Viva. Maybe she told the spiders to come."

"That seems strange," says Wolf worriedly. "I'd better go in and have a look."

Wolf enters the dark cottage, and immediately the smell of sulphur pricks his sensitive nose. It is so dark that he can barely see Viva on the bed. He walks up to her and sniffs gently. Viva also smells faintly of sulphur. Wolf licks her face, but Viva doesn't react. She sleeps deeply, strangely deep.

Wolf looks around the cottage he left just a few hours ago. Spiders and cobwebs are everywhere. He sees them weaving new cobwebs as he watches.

This is black magic, he thinks. *Spiders and sulphur smell! Sigrid better get here quick.*

Wolf turns to two wolves who have followed him inside the house to ask them to fetch Sigrid. Suddenly he hears something outside the cottage and goes to the door. The ravens Ash and Soot are sitting in a tree next to the door, looking at him with worry.

"How is she?" Soot asks. "We felt her calling us and came as soon as we could."

"She sleeps very deep, and it smells like sulphur in the cottage," says Wolf. "We must get Sigrid here."

"Black magic! It's almost the blood moon and evil forces are coming to life," sighs Ash. "Well, we'll fly straight to Nifelheim and bring Sigrid back as soon as we can. In the meantime, you might want to snoop around the cottage and see if you can find anything unusual, but it's best not to touch anything." Ash and Soot take off immediately and fly quickly away towards Nifelheim.

In the treetops, three gray gnomes sit and watch. Gray gnomes are cunning and vicious, always on the lookout for gold and silver.

"Did you hear that?" whispers Trolgar, one of the gray gnomes. "Viva is fast asleep, and there's no one to guard the ellacrosses. We'd better steal them before Sigrid comes and wakes Viva."

"But they said it smells bad in there," whines Botvid. "Remember what it smelled like the last time we went for the ellacross and Tora?"

"Stop whining!" snarls Trolgar who is the leader. "It was Tora who stank, not the ellacross. Let's take the ellacrosses and sell them to Jarl Olav for a lot of money."

The three gray gnomes climb down from the tall trees. Once down on the ground, the Botvid tucks a large clump of green moss into the nostrils of his very large nose. It worked for the stench last time, so it should help here too. Satisfied, he sneaks after his friends towards the cottage with moss hanging out of his big nose.

3

Gray Gnomes and Ellacrosses

The gray gnomes creep cautiously between ferns and bushes, careful not to let the breeze carry their scent to the wolves guarding Viva's cottage. The gray gnomes are armed with thick branches and sharp knives. They creep as close to the cottage as they dare. They watch the wolves and use signs to decide which wolves to go after.

Trolgar nods to the others and they rush forward, screaming wildly as only gray gnomes can. The cry of gray gnomes' cuts through marrow and bone and is unlike anything you've heard before. The wolves cower as the horrific screams suddenly fill the formerly silent clearing. It takes a few seconds for the wolves to react, and that's enough for the gray gnomes. They stab with knives and lash out wildly, and soon three wolves are lying dead or dying outside the cottage.

Wolf, who is inside the cottage with the two wolves named Grey and Black, quickly closes the door. Wolf looks out the small window and sees their friends lying on the ground. The wolves hear the gray gnomes going up on the roof. The chimney rattles, and a few pebbles fall into the ashes.

"What shall we do?" Grey whispers as he leans heavily against the door to keep it closed.

"You two take the gray gnomes that come through the door, and I'll watch the chimney. We'll do the best we can. I'll stand here by the chimney and call for help. If we're lucky, someone will hear our cries," Wolf says, walking over to the big fireplace.

Wolf sticks his head under the chimney so that the sound reaches as far as possible. He takes a deep breath and calls for help. His loud howl hits the walls of the chimney, shaking the stones. The sound grows louder as it goes up through the big chimney and hits the night with tremendous force. There is a strange noise, and then sounds like a large stone rolling down from the roof and landing with a thud.

"What are you doing, you klutz?" sizzles Trolgar at the door to the gray gnomes who has landed with a thud on the ground.

"Oh, my poor ears," says Botvid, holding his gnarled hands over his ears and rocking back and forth. "Just as I was about to climb down the chimney, the ghost howled so loudly that I fell over like a drunken pig in the middle of the day."

"Ghosts! Drunken pigs! What in Thor's name are you talking about? Did you land on your head?" Now Trolgar is so angry he spits when he talks.

"What?" says Botvid, looking at his companion while covering his ears. "I can't hear what you're saying." He confusedly pulls out the moss he has stuffed up his nose and immediately turns green in the face when he smells the stench of sulphur coming from the cottage. Trolgar turns red with anger and pulls his friend's ear so that it almost gets twice as long.

Then they hear a wolf howling in the distance. Someone has heard the cry for help. Suddenly more wolves are howling, and some sound close.

"Now look what you've done!" snarls Trolgar. "More wolves are coming! We've got to get out of here!"

The gray gnomes disappear into the Ancient Forest as fast as they can. None of them want to become supper for a wolf. After a few minutes, help begins to arrive in the clearing. Wolves, foxes, and a couple of moose appear in the darkness to help Viva. Wolf breathes a sigh of relief and goes out to greet his friends.

In the meantime, Ash and Soot have reached Nifelheim. They fly quietly into the great cave hall and land softly on the backs of a couple of chairs. Sigrid sits sleeping in front of the fire, looking tired and worn out. Ash croaks softly a few times, and Sigrid wakes up immediately.

"My friends, what can I do for you?" She looks kindly at the two big black ravens with such clever eyes.

"We come with urgent messages from Wolf. Viva's asleep and they can't wake her. Everything in the cottage is down, and the house is full of cobwebs," says Ash urgently.

"She isn't waking up? Sigrid scratch her nose thoughtfully. "Tell me, did Wolf say anything about a strange smell?"

"Yes, he thinks it smells of sulphur," Soot replies. "We smelled it outside the house when we got close."

"Ok, so we are looking for something inside the cottage, probably near Viva." Sigrid looks at the ravens and asks, "Are you tired, or can you fly back to the cottage?"

"No, we can fly back," the ravens reply together.

"Tell Wolf and his friends to look for a piece of wood with runes burned into it. There will be a very strong smell near the piece of wood so they should be able to sniff it out. But tell them not to touch it! This is very important. We don't know what spells are connected to the runes. Tell them I'll be there as soon as I can. I just need to pick up a few things."

"Okay," say the ravens and fly straight back to the cottage in the Ancient Forest.

Sigrid rushes into her room and gathers the things that might save Viva from eternal sleep. She puts down her large charm made by Thor's hammer, forged by a mighty elf over in the West Woods, a silver box of dragon snuff, a bottle filled with Nix's music, and some fortifying herbs in a bag. She hesitates and then lays down a golden horn, beautifully adorned with runes and diamonds. Then she goes out to find Lita, the dwarfs' guard chief, and the dwarfs who will go to Viva's cottage when dawn breaks.

Away to the east, the sun's rays begin to appear behind the high mountain peaks. Before the first rays of sunlight reach the opening to the great cave hall, Sigrid and the dwarfs are on their way to Viva's cottage. A new day is here.

4

Gealdor with Black Magic

n the clearing of the Ancient Forest, the animals are on guard. More animals have arrived, and sentries are everywhere. It is quiet in the clearing.

Wolf sits by his injured friend lying on the ground as life slowly fades from her eyes. He feels the grief turn to anger and wishes they had caught the gray gnomes. Now he waits for Sigrid and the dwarfs so they can help bury the wolves. Then he will avenge his dead friends.

"Dear friend, I am very sorry for the loss of these fine wolves," says Runar Rat, who has reached Wolf. "A great loss for the forest!"

"Thank you," says Wolf quietly. "When did you get here?"

"I got a lift with a couple of foxes that Sigrid sent away last night," says Runar Rat. "Maybe I can be of some help where you need a smaller creature?"

"Yes, thank you!" says Wolf, trying to get enough energy to help Viva.

Then the two mighty ravens glide across the clearing and land on the roof of the house. They look around and see the dead wolves surrounded by their friends. They quietly jump to the ground and walk up to Wolf.

"A day of sorrow," says Ash.

"Indeed," says Soot, and the two birds stand silent for a moment to think of the dead. "We come with a message from Sigrid. I'm afraid it can't wait. Viva's life may be in danger, and it's urgent."

Wolf nods. "We understand. What does Sigrid say? Come here and listen, friends!"

The animals who are not on guard gather around Wolf and the ravens.

"It's black magic, but you already know that," says Soot. "We're to look for a piece of wood with runes on it. It smells like sulphur, and we can't touch the wood."

"It's very important," says Ash. "Just find the piece of wood, and Sigrid will take care of it."

"Okay, a piece of wood with runes," says Wolf in a loud voice. "It's probably in the cottage. Grey and Black, you're with me—you can sniff a bit higher up. Foxes—you two, Red and Rusty—look down by the floor. And Runar Rat, you take over for the places the rest of us are too big to go. Ready?"

All the animals nod that they understand, and the others immediately start looking for the piece of wood outside the cottage. Inside, the wolves and foxes sniff carefully everywhere so they don't miss anything. The fox Red, searching inside the wardrobe, suddenly calls out, "I think we have something! Whoa, whoa, it smells strong in here."

The entire wardrobe is covered in thick cobwebs. The web sticks to the fox's thick, brownish-red fur as he backs out of the tall cupboard. Red sneezes and sneezes so hard his nose and eyes run.

"Get out in the fresh air for a while," says Wolf. "Runar Rat, it's your turn!"

Runar Rat paws swiftly between the sticky threads of the spider's web and disappears into the cupboard. He follows a very strong smell of sulphur to one corner. He gently lifts a shawl lying twisted around something. There! A brownish-black, rather thick piece of wood with runic writing glowing in yellow red. He drops the shawl and backs out of the cupboard.

"Yep, we found it!" Satisfied, he brushes the dust and cobwebs from his fur. "Now all we can do is wait for Sigrid."

The animals go out of the cottage and sit down to wait. It's not more than a few minutes before Sigrid and the dwarfs arrive. They stop and look surprised. The clearing is practically full of animals of various sizes. There are moose next to wolves, deer next to foxes, birds galore in the trees, rabbits, hares, all crowded there silent, and sad. The beautiful cottage is covered in thick cobwebs that are spreading over the bushes and grass. Hundreds of small birds are trying to pull the cobwebs away, but the web is growing faster than they can remove it.

Sigrid walks up to Wolf, who has returned to stand by his dead friend. She places her hand on the dead wolf, lowers her head, and mutters quietly to herself. Then she stands up and looks kindly at Wolf. "It's a high price you've paid to protect Viva. Thank you!"

"It's the gray gnomes' fault and nobody else's," growls Wolf angrily.

"Revenge is best served cold, my friend," says Sigrid kindly. "When the strongest emotions subside, the best thoughts come. Your dead friends send their regards from the other side and ask you to grieve no more. Now let's make sure they didn't die in vain. Have you found the piece of wood?"

"Yes, it's wrapped in a dirty shawl in the back of the big wardrobe," says Runar Rat. "The runes glow in yellow red."

"There are strong forces at work here," sighs Sigrid. "I ask you dwarfs to start by carrying Viva out and putting her some distance from the cottage."

The dwarfs nod and immediately go into the cottage. Soon after, they bring Viva out and lay her down gently a short distance from the cottage. Two of the dwarfs stand and guard her. Sigrid enters the cottage with Runar Rat. She must cut her way through with a knife because the cobwebs are getting thicker.

She carefully opens the wardrobe door and sticks her head in for a first look. Then she leans out into the room and opens her bag. She pulls out the large charm made by Thor's hammer. Sigrid then takes out her ellacross, which she always wears around her neck. According to the stories about Sigrid and her powers, she met Odin himself when she received her ellacross. Odin is the most powerful of the Aesir gods.

When Sigrid has finished, she leans back into the wardrobe and carefully takes out the piece of wood wrapped in the shawl. There's a little shake from the fabric where Sigrid is holding it. She shudders as she feels the evil forces of the runes trying to seep into her arm, but she keeps rattling off a protective gealdor to herself. Now it is so quiet in both clearing and cottage that you can hear the scrambling of all the spiders weaving their enormous cobwebs.

Sigrid unfolds the shawl so that the piece of board is exposed and she can read the runes.

"Draug sleep!" whispers Sigrid.

The runes sizzle and begin to pulsate in the darkness inside the cottage.

5

New Fala

Tora wakes up and yawns loudly. She looks around the strange room in a daze. Then she remembers that she went to Nifelheim and Sigrid. The feeling of security swirls around her like a warm blanket. She gets up and gets ready for a new day. Then she goes to the large cave hall to see if there is possibly some food.

The cave hall in Nifelheim is usually full of life and chatter, but not today. Everyone is talking about what might have happened to Viva. They are worried about what might happen next. Tora looks for Sigrid and Grim, but there is no sign of them.

"Tora, sit here with me, please," Egil the Dwarf King calls from a table in the middle of the hall.

"Good morning, Egil," says Tora politely. "Has something happened?"

"Good morning, my friend. Yes, I'm sorry. Someone has cast an evil spell, a powerful gealdor, on Viva and her cottage. Sigrid, Grim, and some dwarfs from the guard are there trying to help her. Viva seems to be sleeping very deeply."

Tora is sad when she hears what has happened. Viva, one of the kindest and gentlest women she has ever met, has been bewitched. "I should never have left," says Tora sadly. "I should have stood up and stayed. But no, I just did as Viva said and walked away." Tora starts to cry.

"No tears or regrets," says Egil kindly. "It's good that you did what Viva said. She wouldn't have told you to leave if she didn't think it was necessary. Sigrid is there now, and she knows exactly how to help Viva. We'll have them back here before we even have time to say stomp mush and glutton sausage." Egil pats Tora's arm comfortingly.

"Has it been long since they left? Maybe I can help? After all, I've learned a lot as a seid this summer with Viva." Tora gets up, ready to run all the way to the cottage in the Ancient Forest.

"No, it's not worth it." Egil gently pulls Tora down on the chair again. "They'll probably be back before lunch. I know what you can do in the meantime. You can go and look at New Fala village."

"New Fala village!" Tora looks at him happily. "Is the new village ready?"

"Almost ready. The fire destroyed the clearing where the village was, so we built the new village in a clearing a bit further away. Now the forest can heal the old clearing after the fire. I'll ask some friends to show you the way." Egil stands up and looks across the room. He spots a group of young dwarfs playing Mill game at a table.

"Guys, can you show New Fala village to Tora?" he shouts over the din. "Stay and keep her company, and then make sure she comes back here, please."

"Sure!" The young dwarfs get up, ready to leave immediately.

"Just going to get my bag from my room," says Tora. "Be right back!"

Tora hurries back to the room where she slept. She grabs her jacket and bag, which are lying on a chair. As she lifts the bag, it feels a little heavier than usual. Then she remembers that Viva smuggled something into the bag when she handed it to Tora. Tora sits down on the bed and looks into the bag. At the bottom is an old wooden box.

Tora lifts out the box. She twists and turns it. A beautiful runic script curls around the box, and the wood feels smooth and almost warm in her hands. She has learned runic writing this summer and can read what is written on the box.

"Future bright, with Odin's might," Tora reads aloud. "What does that mean?"

She carefully opens the box. There is thin, red fabric slightly twisted around. She carefully unfolds the fabric. Nine ellacrosses! She has received the last of the ellacrosses in the world.

What will she do now? An ellacross is one of the most powerful things a seid can own, and now she has ten: one around her neck, and nine in her bag. A seid or magician can attach very powerful spells to an ellacross. The cross gives the owner power that should be used with caution.

Tora quickly wraps the ellacross in the fabric and puts it all in the box. She puts the wooden box back in her bag and walks out of the room with firm steps. *Best not to tell anyone. You never know where evil lurks,* Tora thinks.

The crew of young dwarfs are waiting for her on the grassy field in front of the caves.

"I'm Bile and this is Galar and Noss," says one of the dwarfs. "It's not far to the new village."

They go into the forest, and Tora puts the ellacrosses in her bag out of her mind. The youngsters forget to be on their guard and don't see the oknytt hiding up in the trees next to the path. The oknytt look at one another, smile, and nod. They take a deep breath and let out a scream so horrible it defies description.

The leader of the oknytt, Wolfpelt, sits on a rock behind some large ferns in the woods. Ever since his scout told him that Tora had finally left Viva's cottage, he's been honing his plan to steal her ellacross. Wolfpelt has gathered all the oknytt that can be found in the Ancient Forest around the new village that is being built. They hide everywhere, out of sight of anyone walking to and from the construction site. If there's one thing oknytt can do, it's wait patiently for their prey.

The cry of the oknytt bounces among tree trunks and rocks, causing any animal that hears the sound to take cover. Tora and the dwarfs freeze. None of them has heard an oknytt scream. The dwarfs immediately draw their swords, ready to fight for their lives. They stand still and listen intently as they peer into the forest. Then they hear the enemy!

It rattles and paws in all the bushes and thickets. Tora sees branches swaying from the weight of climbers, sees bushes swaying everywhere. But worst of all is the sound of hundreds of feet heading towards them. The dwarfs look at her in fear, and Bile hisses, "Run! Run for all you're worth, Tora!"

Tora hesitates for a brief moment, then turns sharply and starts running back towards Nifelheim. Blood pounding in her ears, she runs like she's never run before.

Then what must not happen happens. She trips on a rock and falls over. She loses her breath and must stay down. Then she sees oknytt a little further along the path, many oknytt. *They're waiting for me! They're blocking the way back to Nifelheim and the help. What am I supposed to do?*

Tora gets up smoothly and runs away from the path, into the woods. She has only one thought in her head: to get as far away as possible from the oknytt chasing her. Just the thought of their leader, Wolfpelt, makes her go cold.

Then the dwarfs' horns echo through the forest. The call for help! Tora knows that anyone in Nifelheim who can hold a sword will try to help the young dwarfs. Suddenly the horns fall silent. Tora doesn't know which is more frightening, the horns' call for help or the silence that now fills the forest.

Tora feels fear creeping through her, and she continues as fast as she can through the forest. She steps over rocks, gets branches in her face, and falls over again and again, but she doesn't stop. She absolutely must not let Wolfpelt get his hands on the ellacrosses. Tired and lonely, Tora continues south through the forest even after night has settled over the woods.

The young dwarfs fight if they can, but the oknytt just keep coming, and finally they must give up. The oknytt force them to the ground while they wait for their master, Wolfpelt. Soon they hear heavy footsteps scurrying along the path. Suddenly two gnarled, dirty feet with long, dirty nails stand in front of the dwarfs' faces.

"Well, what cute little dwarfs," giggles Wolfpelt and pokes them with one foot.

"Keep your dirty foot off us," Galar snarls.

"Well, let's not be grumpy," says Wolfpelt, clicking his tongue. "You should be polite. Didn't your mother teach you that?"

"Lord, we haven't seen the girl," an oknytt stutters nervously, bowing deeply. "No girl."

"Well, maybe it doesn't matter so much," says Wolfpelt thoughtfully.

An oknytt scream of warning is heard over the trees again.

"So, a lot of dwarfs are on their way here," says Wolfpelt. "Good, that must mean that Nifelheim doesn't have so many guards. Okay, hide the dwarfs inside the forest and tell everyone to go to Nifelheim. With any luck, we'll be staying in caves tonight." Wolfpelt laughs so hard his stomach jumps.

6

Oknytt in Nifelheim

When the people of Nifelheim hear the dwarfs' horns in the forest, they spring into action. The dwarf guard is quickly ready, and Egil the Dwarf King sends them away first. Everyone who can fight fetches weapons from the stores deep in Nifelheim. Soon a small army stands on the grassy field in front of the caves.

Egil climbs onto a stone in the middle of the large grassy field. All around him, the clatter of weapons and anxious chatter quickly dies down. The old dwarf looks powerful, calm, and confident as he stands there in beautiful armour that shines in the sun.

"My friends, calm down!" His confident voice reaches everyone. "We don't know what's happened, but we've had reports of a lot of oknytt in the woods over the last few days, so we're not taking any chances. The guards are already on their way, and we'll be leaving soon. Take it easy and think before you do anything! I'll be in the first line, then you all will follow."

Egil jumps to the ground and runs to the edge of the forest. "Sound the march!" he says in a dark, firm voice. The dwarfs' battle horns are heard over the forest for the first time in many, many years.

Egil leads the army into the forest with firm steps. They start jogging, and soon the last dwarfs disappear into the forest. Remaining in Nifelheim are a small guard force and the old, the sick, and all the children. Those not on guard begin to close Nifelheim for safety, but the work is slow. The big doors are not used in peacetime and have not been closed for many years. The task now is to quickly grease the hinges and locks and repair what has broken.

The army of dwarfs moves quickly along the path the youths walked earlier, but they are nowhere to be seen. When the dwarfs reach the clearing and New Fala village, they stop. What now? Egil gathers his closest men around him and addresses them.

"We know that they walked on the path and that they were going to the village, but we don't know if they got all the way here. I suggest we split up so that one group continues ahead on the path on the other side of the village. One group goes back along the path and looks for tracks. Another group spreads out in the woods around the village. Someone must eventually find them or something from them. What do you say?"

The men nod in agreement.

"We know the sounds of our horns, so we will know who's calling from the different signals," says Egil, sorting into scouting parties with a wave of his hand. "Party one, blow once if you find something. Party two, blow twice, and party three, three times."

The dwarfs quickly split into their three scouting parties. Soon the forest around New Fala village is teeming with dwarfs looking for traces of Tora and their missing youths.

Egil sits down on a fallen tree and pulls at the braids of his thick beard in deep thought. He ponders the reports of all the oknytt in the forest and wonders what the sneaky Wolfpelt is up to.

After a while, a dwarf horn blows twice. Egil quickly stands up and starts walking towards the path. *Party two, that's the group that went back towards Nifelheim along the path*, Egil thinks. He immediately starts running back along the path and meets two dwarfs waiting for him.

"In there," they say, pointing into the woods next to the path.

Egil feels an unpleasant lump in his stomach from worry and walks towards the dwarfs standing a little way in. He doesn't really want to go there because who knows what he'll see. But the three young dwarfs are sitting on the ground, rubbing their wrists where they have been bound. Three monk cubs are lying on the moss, and Egil understands that they have not been able to cry for help. But one important person is missing.

"Well, what happened?" Egil asks in a dark voice. "Tell me, where is Tora?"

"We were walking on the path when suddenly oknytt appeared out of nowhere and attacked us. We tried to knock them down but more and more came. Finally, we managed to get the horn up and could blow for help. Then the oknytt took the horn and took us prisoner," Galar says.

"When we saw the oknytt, we shouted at Tora to run away," says Noss, holding Bile's arm for support. "We don't know where she went. She ran back on the path, that's all we know. We don't know if she got away."

"Make sure they get back to Nifelheim, and have someone look at Bile's arm," Egil says. You can hear the anger in his voice.

"I heard a bit of what the oknytt said," says Bile. "I didn't understand everything, but they were looking for Tora and her ellacross. Maybe you know what that means? They mentioned something about Nifelheim too, but I didn't quite hear what they said."

In the meantime, the oknytt have reached the grassy field in front of Nifelheim. They hide in the shadows among the trees while they watch the caves. They have already knocked out some of the dwarf sentries, and they can now plan the attack in peace.

Wolfpelt chuckles quietly to himself. *This is almost better than getting Tora and the ellacross. Imagine sitting on the throne in Nifelheim and receiving Egil, begging for mercy.* Wolfpelt can hardly believe his luck. "Now listen carefully!" he calls to his oknytt. The crowd gathers around their leader. "We make a single attack. There are many of us, and they only have a few guards left. The rest of them can't resist. Do you understand? We all attack at once when I give the order."

The oknytt nod. They are ready to attack Nifelheim.

"Now!" cries Wolfpelt so that saliva splashes around.

All the oknytt rush out of the forest, screaming terribly. The lawn is teeming with the tiny yellowish creatures. Hundreds of long, floppy ears flap about as they climb over one another to try to reach the caves before anyone else. Wolfpelt watches the mess of oknytt wrestling and trampling one another and sighs angrily. "I'm literally surrounded by idiots!" he roars as loud as he can.

His angry roar runs like a current through the oknytt, and they stop fighting each other. The oknytt rush towards Nifelheim. The dwarf guards watch in horror as the beasts pour out of the woods by the hundreds. It takes only a few minutes for the guards to be captured. Nifelheim is in the hands of the oknytt.

Wolfpelt enters the large cave opening with proud, hurried steps and looks around. He could never have dreamed of this; he is the ruler of Nifelheim. Who knows what enormous treasures of gold and silver are hidden in these caves! He almost cries at the thought of all the wealth that is now his.

Wolfpelt scurries to the ancient golden throne where the king of the dwarfs sits for ceremonial feasts or visits. With a contented sigh, he slowly sits on the throne and looks out over the great hall. The room quickly fills with oknytt watching him nervously.

"Welcome to Nifelheim, the caves of the oknytt!" shouts Wolfpelt and slams the walking stick hard into the floor.

Every oknytt in the throne room kneels before their leader as Wolfpelt's evil laughter echoes through the caves.

7

A Strong Gealdor

Runar Rat looks nervously at Sigrid's face, which is lit up by the runes pulsating in a yellow-red glow. Suddenly, he sees the mighty seid behind the friendly woman's face. He now understands the power Sigrid really has over everything living and sometimes over things dead. He becomes very frightened, and a cold chill runs down his back all the way to the tip of his tail. Carefully he clears his throat and says, "I'm sorry, do you know what draug sleep is?" he asks nervously.

Sigrid looks at him blankly at first, then winces and smiles as usual at the rat. "Yes, dear friend, I know. It means sleeping as deeply as a draug, as a living dead. The person can only wake up if you can find the runes and break the spell, the gealdor."

"A living dead! I thought it was just made up," says Runar Rat quietly, looking nervously over his shoulder in the dark cottage.

There is a faint rattle from the spiders as they continue to weave, and the shadows seem to be particularly dark in the corners. Runar wishes with all his heart that he was out in a meadow in the sun instead of in this dark, enchanted cottage.

"Well, don't worry," sighs Sigrid, adjusting the knot of hair on her head. "I know how to break the gealdor. Guard!"

One of the dwarfs who followed from Nifelheim enters through the cobwebs covering the doorway.

"Can you make a fire outside?" asks Sigrid. "Take a lot of firewood to make a strong fire."

"Immediately," replies the dwarf and disappears out again, his beard full of cobwebs.

"Now, my friend, may I ask you to leave," says Sigrid, looking seriously at Runar Rat. "You've been around these runes a little too long. Their power should not be underestimated. Besides, it's dangerous to try to break such a powerful gealdor. Would you please ask everyone to leave the clearing once the fire has taken hold."

"Sure," says Runar Rat and rushes out of the cottage.

He feels tired and sleepy but didn't realize it was from the power of the runes. Once out in the fresh air, he quickly perks up and tells everyone what Sigrid said. Soon only the sleeping Viva and the crackling fire remain in the clearing.

Sigrid comes out of the cottage. She carefully carries the piece of wood wrapped in cloth. The pulsating light from the runes, carved into the wood, reflects on her face. She walks slowly towards the fire. The closer she gets, the slower she walks. Her footsteps in the grass are quickly filled with cobwebs, all the way from the cottage door to the fire. Sigrid keeps rattling a protective gealdor to protect herself from the runes' evil magic.

Bæði ungir og gamlir,
í norðri og suðri,
austur og vestur.
Megi Oden koma,
þegar hans er þörf á sitt besta.

The protective gealdor should be rattled off in Icelandic for extra power, but translated, Sigrid is saying something like this:

Both young and old,

north and south,

east and west.

May Odin come

when he is needed most.

Sigrid stays as close to the fire as she can and looks into the flames. She switches to another gealdor, saying it out loud as she holds the runes above her head.

May the runes burn

and the evil disappear.

May the gods bring life

and keep us safe.

Sigrid slowly makes a counterclockwise turn as she says the gealdor over, and over again. Then she quickly throws the piece of wood with runes on the fire.

The piece of wood seems to be lifted by the flames and hovers just above the burning wood. The wood with runes starts spinning around fast and then suddenly stops. The fire releases an eerie, soft howl, almost like that of the Fenrir wolf.

Bang!

The wood explodes, and the runes float around in the fire for a short while. Then they fall and the fire goes out. Sigrid collapses unconscious on the grass. It is quiet, almost as if the forest is holding its breath waiting for what will happen next.

Suddenly a light comes on inside the little cottage. Darkness begins to disappear in the clearing, and as it gets lighter, the spiders disappear. The cobwebs dissolve into beautiful little dots of light that rise glitteringly towards the treetops. After only a few minutes, all the web is gone, and the sun shines down into the clearing again.

Viva's face has regained its colour, and she is moving around a bit. Runar Rat and Wolf rush up to her as she lies lifeless on the grass. Wolf calls softly to her, and she opens her eyes.

"How did it go? Is she alive?" is the first thing Sigrid asks.

"The runes and the wood are gone, the cobwebs are gone, Viva is awake and as you can feel, the sun is back," says Wolf.

Runar Rat quickly scurries over to Viva and jumps onto her stomach. "Hello, Viva!" he says kindly.

"Hi, Runar," replies Viva tiredly. "Thanks for getting me back!"

"Say thanks to Sigrid!" says Runar, pointing to where Sigrid is getting up wearily. "The rest of us didn't do much."

Sigrid walks over to Viva and kneels beside her. "My friend, I wasn't sure I'd be able to get you back. There was very strong magic in the runes."

"Thank you, I know how hard it was for you," Viva says, patting Sigrid on the cheek.

"Do you know who did this?" Sigrid asks.

"Yes, bad times are ahead," whispers Viva. "He'll be at his strongest at the blood moon. By then we'll need to have gathered enough strength to stop him." Viva takes hold of Sigrid's arm so tightly it hurts.

"Who are you talking about that is so evil and strong?" whispers Sigrid.

Just then, the scream of the oknytt is heard through the forest, fainter but still horrifying. Sigrid and Viva freeze and listen. The evil times seem to be here already.

"Oknytt?" Sigrid asks in surprise.

"Their battle cry," says Viva. "But what will they attack?"

Then they hear the dwarfs' horns faintly in the wind. Sigrid stands up and looks at the dwarfs from the guard. "We need to get back as soon as we can. They may need my help." Sigrid takes a few steps but stumbles to a halt from fatigue.

"You're too tired to run back," says the watch commander. "We'll run ahead so you two can stay here with the wolves as guards."

"Sounds wise," Wolf says quietly to Sigrid. "We'll watch over you while you rest."

"Okay," says Sigrid, "it's a plan."

Then the dwarfs' battle horns blast over the forest.

"Battle horns! The call to battle hasn't been heard for many years," says the watch commander, looking worried. "We must go home!" The dwarfs run out of the clearing and disappear towards Nifelheim.

"Say, you didn't bring some dragon snuff?" Viva asks. "I think I'm going to need some to get my strength back."

"Yes, I took my silver box with me, in case you needed it." Sigrid helps Viva up, and they walk arm in arm into the cottage.

The animals outside soon see smoke curling from the chimney, and candles are lit in the window again. Everything is back to normal in the clearing. Wolf sits down in front of the door, and the other animals spread out in the clearing and the forest to keep watch.

8

WOLFPELT AND EGIL THE DWARF KING

Wolfpelt sits on the throne and yells at the poor oknytt who have the misfortune to work inside the halls of Nifelheim. He wants more mead, more food, more cakes. There's never an end to it. Wolfpelt doesn't dare leave the throne in the great throne room even for a few minutes. What if Egil the Dwarf King is sitting there when he comes back?

Wolfpelt knows it won't take long before Egil understands where all the oknytt have gone. They've probably found the dwarfs tied up in the forest by now. Wolfpelt expects the dwarf army to be outside the doors soon. The oknytt have closed and locked the big doors that the dwarfs hadn't had time to close. Wolfpelt feels quite safe inside the great hall.

One of the first things Wolfpelt did when they arrived in Nifelheim was to send out oknytt to look for dwarfen gold in the caves. By all accounts, most of the dwarfs' vast wealth is in Nifelheim, safe and impossible to steal. But Wolfpelt is going to try.

Then he hears a horn outside. The dwarfs have come home. Wolfpelt feels the fear run like cold water down his back even though he is behind the locked doors. He is used to stealing coins and silver bowls, but not the dwarfs' home. He is beginning to realize that he has done something very foolish.

He goes to one of the big doors and opens the small flap in the door. Outside, dwarfs stand in rows as far as he can see. Right in front of the hatch, Egil the Dwarf King stands with his hands at his sides, looking very angry. "Wolfpelt, you old rat's nest! What are you up to?" Egil asks.

"But hey, Egil! So nice of you to visit. Would you like to come in for a glass of mead?" Wolfpelt asks, stalling.

"I'll give you a horn of mead if you don't stop this nonsense at once," Egil snarls. "Get out of Nifelheim right now!"

"Well," says Wolfpelt cunningly, "we'll just find the gold first. Then you can have your cold caves back."

Egil stands silently staring at the dirty leader, thinking of all the oknytt running around and fouling his caves.

"Okay, but I can show you where the gold is," says Egil, suddenly looking friendly. "Then you can go home."

Wolfpelt can't believe it. Egil will show him where the gold is? This sounds too good to be true. He decides to let Egil in and see what happens. "How nice of you," says Wolfpelt in a silly voice that turns dark. "But only you!"

Wolfpelt opens the heavy door just enough for Egil to squeeze in. What Wolfpelt doesn't know is that dwarfs always have secret passageways so they can go in and out of their homes unseen. Dwarfs have benefited from these many times. The passageways in Nifelheim are vast and have many hidden entrances.

When Egil had realized that Wolfpelt had tricked him and entered Nifelheim, he sent half the army around the mountain to the enter where the oknytt would never see them. The dwarfs are already pouring into Nifelheim, hiding in position and wait for his signal. And some dwarfs have received a special order from the dwarf king.

Egil squeezes through the door that Wolfpelt holds ajar and then adjusts his armour. "So Wolfpelt, you've started playing tricks."

"Well," says Wolfpelt, feeling a little flattered, "I saw an opportunity and took it, plain and simple. Now, show me the way to your vast treasures."

"Absolutely," says Egil kindly. "This way!"

Egil takes a torch and starts to go further into the cave. Wolfpelt hesitates for a second before following. It's a bit strange that the dwarf king has given up so easily. He'd better be on his guard.

They continue deeper into the cave along dark winding passageways. Down and down, and Wolfpelt begins to realize just how big Nifelheim really is.

At last, Egil stops in front of a door with a large lock that glitters gold in the torchlight. He lights the torches hanging on either side of the door. "We're here," he says, looking pleased.

"Okay," says Wolfpelt hesitantly. "Is all your gold behind this little door?"

"Yes. You see what an expensive and large lock we have on the door." Egil points to the golden lock that looks brand new, which in fact it is. The dwarfs who received the special order from Egil have replaced the old broken lock on this door with a large new one covered in purest gold. They don't usually need to lock the door to the treasures because nobody wants or dares to go in there. (Luckily, dwarfs always have a stock of things that might be useful. Locks are one such thing.)

"Shall we unlock it?" Egil asks, taking down the key that is hanging on a nail on the wall.

"Yes, but you go in first," says Wolfpelt, still suspicious of the cunning dwarf.

Egil unlocks the door and hangs the key on the nail again. He tries to open the door, but it is stuck. "You'll have to help," says Egil as he strains to push open the heavy door.

Wolfpelt sees that the door is stuck and comes to stand next to Egil. Egil counts to three, and they push with all their might. The door opens, and Wolfpelt falls into the dark room. Egil, holding the door handle, remains standing in the doorway. He lights the torch hanging on the wall. "Now you can have it your way," Egil says in a cold and angry voice. "Your dream is coming true. Welcome to our treasure chamber! Here are our finest diamonds and our most beautiful gold."

"Oh," says Wolfpelt when he sees the shining gold.

Then there is a rattle further into the darkness of the cave, and a loud snort. Wolfpelt freezes. "What … what was that sound?" he asks, peertin into the shadows.

"Oh, did I forget to tell you?" Egil says, looking coldly at the oknytt sitting on the floor amid the treasure. "Because the things in this room are so valuable, we have two dragons guarding it. Sour beasts!"

"Dragons?" Wolfpelt whispers and quickly tries to stand up. "Two dragons?"

"Well, they are so small, so we thought it was best that there were two of them. They keep each other company in the dark. Their names are Moin and Goin, if you want to talk to them. Well, I must go, but have fun with all the gold." Egil steps out and starts closing the door.

Wolfpelt feels a panic coming on. "Wait! I'm sorry, I didn't mean any harm. I don't want your gold."

The terrified leader of the oknytt tries to get up but stumbles and can't reach the door before it closes with a thud that echoes in the cave. He hears the dwarf turn the key, and then there is silence. He crouches by the door and tries to see into the shadows the torch casts along the walls. Then he hears a snort, closer this time.

9

Tora's Escape

Tora has walked almost all night, until she can't walk anymore. Hungry and thirsty, she decides to get some sleep. She lies down under a large spruce tree with dense branches. The thick branches of the tree protect her from prying eyes and the rain that comes during the night. She dreams but she doesn't understand the dreams.

Tora spins around in the dream. Suddenly her grandmother appears. She grabs Tora and shakes her gently. Grandma looks Tora in the eye and says in a firm, deep, voice, "Wake up, Tora!"

Tora wakes up with a jolt. The dream lingers and is so real that Tora almost expects her grandmother to be standing there beside her. Then she hears grunts and snorts out on the path, and she smells a foul stench. It smells worse than the ellacross when evil forces approach. Out on the path, she hears some whiny voices. One wails, "Oh no, such a stench! It stings my nose and eyes."

"Then maybe we are on the right track. It should stink when you are close to the girl."

Tora peers cautiously between the branches of the spruce tree. She sees two gray gnomes standing there, clasping their big noses with their gnarled hands. They look around to see if they can find any trace of Tora.

How lucky it rained last night, Tora thinks, hoping the rain washed away her tracks.

Then a bush creaks, and the branches bend away. Two skunks come out onto the path with their tails raised over their backs. The animals are ready to spray the smelly defensive weapon they have in their backs. "Leave or we'll spray you," one of the skunks snarls.

"The smell cannot be washed away," snarls the other skunk. "You'll smell disgusting for months if you don't run back to where you came from!" He flexes his butt to spit on one of the gray gnomes.

"Sorry to bother you!" says Trolgar the gray gnome, and then to his friend Botvid, "Let's go!" They run back along the path.

"It wasn't Tora, it was the skunks that smelled!" shouts Trolgar as he rushes after his friend.

The skunks stay on the path until they can't hear the gray gnomes anymore. Then they lower their tails and crawl under the tree to join Tora.

"Hi Tora," says one of the skunks. "My name is Scent, and this is my sister Rose."

"Hello," says Tora politely. "Nice to meet you! How do you know who I am?"

"Viva and Sigrid have asked everyone in the forest to help you if needed. We saw you crawl under the tree last night. We stayed behind and kept watch while you slept," says Rose.

"When we saw the disgusting gray gnomes crawling along the path with their noses on the ground," explains Scent, "we thought it was time for us to help. No one stays behind when we spray the special liquid we have at the tail." Scent laughs as she remembers how people have run away screaming, afraid of being sprayed.

"Thank you! It's a good thing you were here," Tora says, crawling forward and standing up. "Now I must go." Tora feels the panic slowly coming and the urge to run so far away as possible.

"Where are you going? Might be good for us to know in case Sigrid asks," says Scent.

"I'm going south and staying away until things calm down," says Tora, looking sad.

"Are you walking alone?" Rose asks. "Aren't you going to wait for Wolf?"

"Anyone who is close to me or tries to help me is in trouble. It's better that I go alone."

"We understand," says Rose, nodding. "Follow the path and you'll come to a lake and the town of North Island. People from all over live there, and many travel there to buy and sell goods. No one will notice a newcomer there."

"But it's quite a long way," says Scent. "It takes a while to get to the ferry that goes out to North Island. The boat is free and takes you to the town, which is on an island in Lake North. That's why the town is called North Island."

"Thank you for your help!" says Tora.

She walks a few steps on the path before turning around and waving to the skunks who are still watching her. Then she disappears along the path, heading south to the town of North Island. Now that she knows where she's going, she feels a little better.

Meanwhile, Viva and Sigrid sit across from each other at the table in the old cottage. They close their eyes and hold each other's hands as they rattle a chant together. The flame of the only candle lit in the cottage flickers as the two mighty seids say the chant louder and louder.

> Let us see,
> where she might be.

Suddenly the light goes out, and the seids fall silent. The cottage is dark, and the only thing they hear is the mice skittering on the floor.

Poof! The candle lights up again on its own, and Viva and Sigrid look at each other. They sit quietly for a long time, then relax and smile at each other.

"Good," sighs Viva. "She's safe, and we know where she's going."

"Best not to say it out loud," says Sigrid. "We don't know who's listening."

"True. I think we'll search the cottage thoroughly tomorrow to make sure no spiders have stayed behind to spy." Viva looks around.

"Good suggestion! It's always good to tidy up sometimes. I'm just going to go out and have a little chat with Wolf and the ravens. Will you make some tea in the meantime?"

Sigrid goes out and closes the door carefully behind her. She signals to Wolf and the ravens that she wants to talk to them. She bends down to whisper quietly first to Wolf, then to the ravens. Wolf and the ravens nod that they understand and immediately set off south through the forest.

They don't see the spiders that suddenly appear on the roof of the cottage and quickly make their way to the ground. But Sigrid sees them and smiles. *I think it's time for me to throw a protective spell over this cottage.* She opens the door and goes into the warmth where the tea is waiting.

10

Nortn Island

Tora stands on the shore and looks out over the great lake called North. The water is like a mirror, and the mist dances just above the surface. The ferry that runs back and forth between the beach and the island is slowly approaching. The ferry docks and opens the gates for unloading. Tora hasn't seen so many people for days, and she's starting to feel safe. No one will notice her among all these people.

Once the ferry is unloaded, it's time for new passengers to board. First, the caged geese, grunting pigs led by strings, and clucking hens are loaded. Then the people board, the gates are closed, and the ferry is off again.

Tora looks up at the blue sky and lets the autumn sun warm her face. She sees three black birds flying in large circles high above the water. She thinks of the ravens and her grandmother. Just then, one of the birds flies slowly down towards the ferry and lands quietly and gracefully on one of the masts.

The raven shakes its feathers and stretches its wings. He looks down at the passengers who don't notice the bird. Well, one passenger sees the raven. Soot has landed on the ferry, and Ash and Black are flying high above. *That means Sigrid knows where I am. Oh, I hope Wolf shows up soon*, Tora thinks. *But how will he get to the island? He can't go by the ferry.*

Tora looks along the beach to see if Wolf is around, but the shore is empty. Soot the raven keeps her company on the ferry until it docks at the jetty in the town of North Island, then flies off as Tora disembarks with the other passengers. She goes to the side and looks around. She doesn't know where to go now.

The passengers and animals that came with the ferry disappear into alleys leading away from the port. People are loading and unloading goods from the houses along the quay to boats and wagons. It smells good of various spices from large sacks that lie along one of the houses and Tora suddenly gets hungry.

The ravens are nowhere to be seen. Tora decides to go into one of the most crowded alleys. She must squeeze through because there are so many humans, dwarfs, and elves in a delightful mix. People are talking, shouting, and laughing, and everywhere people are trying to sell their products.

After a while, Tora comes out into a large square. In the square, there is row after row of market stalls full of goods. It seems you could buy everything you might ever need and then some. Tora walks up and down the rows, looking curiously. Every time she passes someone selling food, she gets a taste in her hand. Soon she has enough food to last her a few days.

Tora sits down on a bale of straw by a wall and eats a piece of bread she was given. In the worst case, she could sleep here on the straw bale tonight. As she sits eating and watching the people, she hears a faint voice and feels someone pulling her by the pants.

"Hello!"

Tora looks down at the straw bale. A very cute little mouse is sitting there looking at her with its gingerbread-brown eyes. Tora holds out her hand for the mouse to jump onto. She gently lifts the mouse to the level of her face.

"Hello!" says the mouse a little nervously. "May I ask what your name is?"

"Hi, I'm Tora. What's your name?"

"My name is Pepper, and I know Sigrid. Welcome to North Island!"

"Thank you very much!" Tora is beginning to understand how practical it is to be able to talk to animals.

"I'll show you where you can sleep tonight. I live in a warm stable myself, and the horse has said that you are welcome there too. We've got you a pair of scissors, just as Sigrid said," says Pepper in an eager voice, "but what do you need scissors for?"

"To cut my hair short, so people think I'm a boy," Tora says. Sigrid thinks of everything. Her curly hair has grown quite long over the summer. "My name will be Tore from now on."

"Ok," says the mouse. "You humans are a bit weird, *Tore*." She giggles. "If you take me in your hand, I'll show you the way to the stables. It'll be dark soon, and I'm sure you're tired."

Tora and Pepper walk along the houses, down a narrow alley that smells of manure and through a stable door. Inside it is warm and smells of hay and straw. A large workhorse nods welcomingly to Tora. Pepper shows her where to sleep, and Tora sits down with a sigh on a bale of straw. It feels safe and warm here. She takes the scissors lying on the straw bale and starts cutting off her hair.

On the other side of the lake, Wolf stands and smells, but there are too many scents in the air for him to smell Tora. He has run the distance from the clearing to North Island as fast as he can. Next to him, Ash sits on a rock. They think about how Wolf will get to the island, but they can only think of one way. He must swim, but it's quite far, and the water isn't very warm.

"Only do it if you're absolutely sure you can make it," Ash says anxiously.

"I can if I take it easy," says Wolf. "I might as well swim over right away." The wolf goes out into the cold water and begins the long swim out to North Island.

11

Unexpected Visit

In Nifelheim they are having a big clean-up. The oknytt have made a terrible mess, looking for gold and jewellery. They seem to have been everywhere, pulling things out, dirtying and smashing things. Egil the Dwarf King sits on his throne. He's so angry he almost has fumes coming out of his ears.

Now they'll fix the big doors and locks so the dwarfs can quickly close Nifelheim in case of danger. They will check and clean up all secret passages so that dwarfs can escape in or out quickly and safely. Food, water, weapons, and torches must be kept in reserve in various places in the caves, and all dwarfs must know where everything is.

Egil gives new orders all the time, and the dwarfs work as fast as they can because no one feels safe anymore. What evil forces are on their way as both oknytt and gray gnomes grow bolder by the day? There have also been sightings of glutton hogs and even mountain giants on the edge of the Ancient Forest.

Egil sends a messenger to the other dwarf cities with orders to prepare for war. He also calls the leaders to a war ting, a council on preparing for war. They are to come to Nifelheim, but they must be careful when they travel. Neither gray gnomes nor Wolfpelt must get wind of the meeting.

The dwarf king rises from his throne and asks some guards to accompany him down to the treasure chamber. It's time to see what's happened to Wolfpelt, trapped in the dark with the two dragons. He brings two large beeswax cakes filled with sweet golden-yellow honey, because that's what dragons are crazy about.

They go deep into the mountain and stop outside the door with the new golden lock. Egil takes the key from the nail next to the door and turns it. The lock opens with a faint click. Egil pushes the door open wide and shines a torch inside. The floor nearest the door is empty except for Wolfpelt's worn coat, which lies half-burnt in one corner.

Egil enters the room and lifts the coat. The thick fabric is still smoking, but Wolfpelt is nowhere to be seen. The guards enter with more torches, and they shine as far into the treasure chamber as they can. As the light reaches further in, they hear snorting in the depths of the cave, and a rattle and clatter among the gold and coins as the dragons climb towards the dwarfs.

The dwarfs listen for any sign of life from Wolfpelt, but all they hear is the snorting of the dragons as they make their way across the riches towards the door.

"We'd better get out," says Egil, and throws what's left of Wolfpelt's coat into one corner.

Egil puts the beeswax cakes on the floor and quickly leaves the treasure chamber. He closes the door behind him, locks it, and hangs the key on the wall again. Egil bows his head in a short prayer for Wolfpelt. "Poor Wolfpelt! But he was stupid to think he could take over Nifelheim. I hope Odin accepts his soul."

The dwarfs bow their heads and mutter after him, "I hope Odin accepts his soul."

They start walking back to the throne room. There are a few loud thumps on the door, then silence again in the cavernous passage deep in the mountain.

In the meantime, it's business as usual in the little cottage in the clearing in the Ancient Forest. Viva is very tired, and Sigrid can see how the draug sleep has taken its harsh toll on her. Viva grows more tired and paler with each passing day. No matter what fortifying stews Sigrid cooks, nothing seems to help.

Viva pats Sigrid's arm reassuringly as Sigrid puts out another cup of tea. "Better put on some more tea water, my friend. And get out the honey, sour milk, and linen strips, because we're going to have visitors soon," Viva says, blowing on the hot tea.

"If you say so, it will be so." Sigrid trusts Viva's premonitions and inner visions.

Sigrid pours water into the teapot and hangs it on the hook over the fire. Then she puts honey and sour milk on the table.

"Can you handle a visit, Viva?" Sigrid looks at her anxiously. "You look tired."

"We can handle this visit, even if it's unexpected," says Viva. "Someone with a burning wound needs our help."

The ladies sit quietly at the table, drinking tea and waiting for the visitor. It is not long before there is a gentle knock on the door. Sigrid gets up and opens the door. She can't see who it is because the person has a blanket over their head.

"Good day, I need your help as a healer," says a raspy voice. "I pray!"

"Of course," says Sigrid, opening the door wide. "Please, you're expected."

The tall, hunchbacked man limped into the cottage and bows politely to Viva. Sigrid pulls out a chair. "Sit down and tell us what we can do for you."

The man sits down with a groan of pain. The blanket slides down his shoulders, and Sigrid sees the burns on his face, neck and one hand.

"We will help you," says Viva. "It will take time for the wounds to heal, and you will have scars. Unfortunately, the dragon fire scars will always hurt."

"Thank you," says the man. "I'll pay whatever it costs if you help me." The man puts some gold coins on the table with his healthy hand.

"We don't want the dwarfs' coin, Wolfpelt," says Viva. "We want you to promise from now on not to steal or cheat anymore."

Wolfpelt nods and promises.

12

Jarl Olav and Guest

In the great castle in the town of Silje, Jarl Olav restlessly wanders his great hall. He has noticed that people have changed since Tora managed to escape from the castle. They are not so afraid of him anymore. Sometimes they laugh at him when they think he can't hear. It will be a long time before people forget how he had to run to the outhouse after eating Tora's cursed porridge.

"Damn you, useless gray gnomes!" shouts Jarl Olav, kicking a basket of apples on the floor. "I must get Tora or an ellacross. With an ellacross, I can make my own gold and be as rich as the dwarfs. Or even richer."

Jarl Olav hisses and mutters and kicks everything he can get his hands on. Soon there are no animals or people left in the great hall—except for one rat who has climbed up on a beam in the ceiling. Up there, in the shadows, Tailtip listens to everything that is said in the hall.

Jarl Olav earns a lot of money every month at the market in town, but a man like him is never satisfied. Jarl Olav always wants more and will never be truly happy. He goes down to the treasure chamber under the castle every day. There he looks at all the money and runs his hands through it, but he is still sad and lonely.

He throws himself down on a chair in the great hall and starts drumming his fingers hard on the table. A servant peers cautiously into the room, plucks up courage, and enters.

"Excuse me, Jarl Olav," he says so quietly that you almost can't hear what he's saying.

"What do you want?" Jarl Olav asks, looking sourly at the poor servant as he grabs a cookie from a plate.

"You have a visitor, sir," says the servant, bowing deeply.

"Well, don't just stand there, man! Let him in!" shouts Jarl Olav angrily. But really he thinks it's quite nice to have visitors. It's been a while since anyone dared to come to the castle.

The servant quickly disappears from the room to fetch the visitor. Out in the great hall stands an old man with a long white beard, his back bent with pain. He is leaning on a gnarled walking stick, so worn that the wood has been sanded smooth and soft. Around his lean body hangs a beautiful black cloak adorned with branches, leaves, and runes in shimmering gold threads.

The elderly man walks slowly into the hall. All that can be heard is the crackle of the large fireplace and the thump of the walking stick as it hits the floor.

Thump. Thump. Thump.

The man walks up to Jarl Olav and bows. "A pleasure, my king," he greets him politely.

"Finally, a person who knows how to greet me," Jarl Olav says with a sigh. "Who are you, my good sir? May I ask your name?"

"My name is Birk," the old man replies, bowing again. "I'm passing through and ask for a place to sleep and preferably a bite to eat."

"You're brave, daring to go to the king himself to beg for food." Jarl Olav laughs. He immediately loses interest in the man when he realizes he is a beggar.

The old man mumbles something to himself and makes a small movement with his hand. It glistens as if he has thrown sand in the sunshine, and Jarl Olav stretches.

"But of course you can," he says, pointing to a chair. "Sit down and I'll feed you right away. Food!" he shouts as loud as he can.

The old man called Birk sits down at the table and takes off his thick cloak. Under the cloak is a black and gold tunic, so beautiful that Jarl Olav can't stop looking at it. The pattern of gold threads seems to be alive and changing shape all the time.

Soon the table is full of food, fruit, cookies, and mugs full of mead. Jarl Olav and his guest eat, talk, and enjoy themselves together while the rat listens above their heads. When dinner is over, Jarl Olav orders a room to be prepared for the guest.

"No, I'll sleep in your room," says Birk calmly.

"My room?" Jarl Olav looks surprised. "But where will I sleep?"

Birk makes the same gesture with his hand and Jarl Olav changes his mind at once. "Move my things to another room immediately!"

The servants look at one another in surprise, not sure if Jarl Olav is joking with them, but an order is an order. They quickly move all the jarl's things to a smaller room a bit further down the corridor. Birk slowly enters the jarl's room and looks around with satisfaction.

"That'll do for now," says Birk, slamming the door with a thud that can be heard through half the castle.

Up on the rafter, Tailtip scratches his stomach thoughtfully and thinks, *This can't be good. Not good at all! I'd better send a message to Sigrid.* The rat scurries off along the rafters and into the castle courtyard to ask someone to fly to Sigrid with a message.

Jarl Olav sits confused in his new room among all the things that have just been put together in a mess. His favourite blanket, his pillow, books, clothes, shoes, even his stool are in a pile on the floor. He's not sure what happened. He's been thrown out of his own room by a man he doesn't know. He lies down on the bed with a deep sigh.

13

WOLF, TORE, AND TRULS

Wolf stumbles onto the beach, exhausted after the long swim and nearly frozen. He lies still for a few minutes and rests before slowly getting to his feet. He shakes his coat thoroughly to make it as dry as possible. The wolf stretches his legs, letting the tired muscles stretch and then relax.

The ravens sit and watch a bit away. They look at the wolf, and Wolf silently signals for them to leave. The ravens fly low between the houses and show Wolf the way to the stable where Tora is sleeping. The big door is closed for the night, so Wolf curls up along the wall of the house. The tired wolf falls asleep immediately. The ravens sit on the rooftops in the alley to rest and keep watch.

The town slowly wakes up as the sun rises over the rooftops. Wolf stretches and sits down to wait for the door to the stable to open. It's not long before it creaks open a bit and Tora slips out into the alley. She stops short when she spots Wolf.

"But how did you get here, my friend?" Tora hugs the wolf. "You're all wet. Don't tell me you swam all the way?"

"Yes, it was no problem," says Wolf, stretching a little proudly. "A bit cold, perhaps."

"You could have drowned! Don't do that again," Tora says sternly as she pats her friend.

"You've cut your hair again, I see," says Soot from the roof. "So, what will 'Tore' do today?"

"Yes, I am Tore from now on. It feels safest. I thought I'd see if I could make some money divining people at the market in the square. Then I thought I'd collect some herbs and sell herbal tea for headaches and other ailments. I'll stay here in town as long as I can."

"Sounds good," says Wolf. "Maybe we can ask some friends to keep an eye out for a room for you to stay in? The stables are nice, but it's better to have a room."

"That's what we do," says Tora. "Let's go to the market and see if I can make some money today."

Tora walks eagerly towards the square. She peers along the aisles and decides on a corner where a large alley leading from the ferry meets the main square. There she pulls together some straw bales and begins to do business. People are happy to pay a penny to have their questions about the future answered. Tora has already made quite a bit of money by the time lunchtime rolls around.

As a seid, she can often see the future of people by taking their hands and closing her eyes. She can't explain what's happening, but she sees the person's future as if in a blurry dream. Whether the prediction comes true depends on what the person then does. Fate usually listens to good deeds, but bad deeds can change the future several times.

Most customers ask about simple things, like whether they should buy the pig they looked at, or does a certain person love me. Tora usually tells the truth, but sometimes it's best not to tell the person everything she sees. No one needs to know in advance about illness and death because there's nothing you can do about it. This afternoon Tora is going out to collect herbs for her teas. Then she can sell herbal tea to those who need help.

After just a few days, word of the talented boy who can tell fortunes and brew soothing teas has spread through the town. The queue at Tora's straw bales is long, and she enjoys it. She feels like she is doing something useful and helping the people of the town. Wolf lies beside her and watches everyone who comes up, ready if anyone seems dodgy. Sometimes people ask what breed the dog is because it is so big and powerful. Tora usually mutters something about it being a mix. Wolf usually snorts contemptuously to himself.

One day, Tora notices an older man in a beautiful red cloak with white leather trim, standing there watching as she works. When the last customer of the day has happily left to buy the pig, as Tora has said to, he slowly comes up to her. Wolf looks at the man with his cold, yellow-black eyes and growls. The man raises his hand and says kindly, "Take it easy, Wolf, I won't hurt her."

Tora looks at the man in surprise, and Wolf quickly gets up, ready to jump on him if necessary.

"How do you know what I am?" Wolf asks, wondering whether the man really can talk to animals.

"I've heard about you two," says the man, sitting down on one of the straw bales. "I'll call you Tore because you chose to be here in North Island. Viva and Sigrid are old acquaintances of mine. When I heard rumours about the talented young man in the square, I thought I'd better have a look."

"You know our names," Tora says, still wary. "What's yours?"

"Sorry, that's rude of me," says the man, bowing slightly. "I am called Truls. I am the chief's healer and advisor here in North Island. Our chief is now old and tired, and I mostly make potions to ease the aches and pains in his worn-out body."

"I can't remember Sigrid and Viva telling me anything about a man called Truls," says Tora.

"No, it's been a long time since we met. For example, I know that Sigrid's good friends Ash, Soot, and Black are sitting on the rooftop over there watching us."

The ravens nod to Tora, and she relaxes a little. It seems that Truls Healer can be trusted for now.

"I have a suggestion, Tore," says Truls, smiling warmly. "I have a small shop in my house where I sell ointments and teas. There is also a small room with a bed that is currently vacant. You can sleep there safely, and we can help each other run the shop. What do you say?"

Tora looks at Wolf, who nods. It sounds wonderful to have a roof over our heads, a fireplace, and a bed to sleep in. Tora smiles broadly and accepts the offer. She gathers her things, and they walk towards the north side of the square where Truls' home is.

14

Weapons and Beacons

Things are happening in the big forest. The New Fala village is ready. A line of people carrying stuff and furniture between Nifelheim and the new village winds through the trees. Everyone who can helps, and soon the things that were saved from the fire are moved to the new village. Sigrid stands leaning against her cane, looking at the beautiful village up in the treetops. She is filled with joy as she sees people walking everywhere. Soon candles are lit in the windows, and smoke comes from the chimneys.

She feels like she's home again, even though it's a new village in a new place. She belongs here, in the village as chief and leader. When word came to Viva's cottage that the village was ready, she left, but Viva was joined by a couple of white elves who came to visit. The white elves have promised to stay with her for a while. *Maybe they can help her more than I can*, Sigrid thinks.

It's a good thing the village was finished just now because Nifelheim is full of dwarfs from both north and south. They have come for the Dwarfen War Ting, the meeting where they will talk about how to prepare for war. Sigrid finds it sad that they are preparing for war, but at the same time she understands. Wolfpelt made his way into Nifelheim, all the way into the treasury, and Egil the Dwarf King will not forget that as long as he lives.

She starts walking up the stairs that wind around the sturdy tree. She goes into her new house and closes the door with a sigh. Soon there is a knock on the door.

"Hello in the cottage," calls out Grim Dwarf, taking a cheerful leap over the threshold. "But how nice! You've already had time to get cosy." Grim pulls out a chair at the table and sits down.

"But hello, Grim," says Sigrid. "It's been a while since we saw each other."

"Yes, it's been full steam ahead with the rumours and war talk and preparations both day and night. I hope the leaders are taking it easy and waiting to see what happens," Grim sighs with concern.

"Yes, it's always good to think twice before you do something," says Sigrid. "Do you know what they've decided?"

"No, but our guests are going back home. That's good, I guess. How are you?" Grim asks, looking worriedly at Sigrid. "You look a bit tired."

"Thank you, I'm fine, but Viva is not feeling well. The white elves are with her now. I hope they can do something. The evil gealdor cast on her nearly killed her."

"I'm so sorry to hear that. Do you know who did it? Brage doesn't have the skill for that. And where is Tora? I haven't seen her in a while." Grim looks questioningly at Sigrid.

"She is safe with an old friend of mine. She'd better stay there for a while. Are you going to Egil's for a chat? Maybe we'll find out what the dwarfs decided on their war ting."

The two friends set off for Nifelheim. On the lawn in front of the caves there are now guards day and night. Some doors are closed, and others are guarded. There is hammering and smithing everywhere. Swords, helmets, and armour stand in rows, waiting to be put in the dwarfs' stores in the caves. Everything that is carried into the caves is carefully written down in long lists so that you know exactly what is there. In the middle of all the mess, Egil the Dwarf King stands looking pleased.

He spots Sigrid and Grim and gives them a friendly wave. "Welcome! As you can see, we are making weapons. The caves are secured and can now withstand an attack if Wolfpelt should decide to do it again."

"There are worse and more cunning enemies than oknytt, I'm afraid," Sigrid says. *It will be a long time before we hear about Wolfpelt again,* Sigrid thinks.

"Well, now the war ting is over. We've decided some good things, so I feel calmer now," says Egil, patting his slightly too round belly with satisfaction. "Soon my friends from the north will be heading home to prepare the same way we are. All the beacons are ready so we can quickly warn each other."

"What beacons?" Sigrid asks.

"We have built fires on ridges and mountaintops from here all the way to the northern dwarf village. If anything happens, we light the beacons, the fires, in a long chain so the warning gets through quickly and we can prepare our defences. We used to do that when the Vikings came, and it worked very well. Now we'll continue to build beacons all over Nordanland."

The people on the grassy field fall silent and watch as the dwarfs from the north march out of Nifelheim in two proud ranks. They stop at the same time as if on cue, turn their heads to Egil and salute. Then they march off tactfully as the sun shines on their well-worn helmets. Egil enjoys seeing how well trained the dwarfs are.

Over in the woods, the two gray gnomes Trolgar and Botvid sit high up in an old spruce tree. They see the dwarfs marching home and look at each other. Tora is not here in Nifelheim. It is time to go to Jarl Olav and tell him what they have seen and heard. They slip quietly down the thick trunk of the spruce and set off for the town of Silje and the castle.

15

Birk and the Gray gnomes

Inside the great hall of Silje castle, Birk sits on the throne. Jarl Olav himself sits on a small rickety old stool. The servants whisper and chatter about all the strange things that are happening in the castle since Birk arrived. The food never runs out, the big barrels are always full of mead, and the candles never burn down. Jarl Olav does exactly as the man says, without whining. That alone is very strange.

Birk calls for a servant. "Summon the leader of the gray gnomes. Tell him to come at once!"

Birk makes his movement with his hand, it glitters, and the servant immediately feels that he must get the leader of the gray gnomes here at all costs. He rushes out of the hall and into the castle courtyard and *bang*, collides with two gray gnomes. The gray gnomes are on their way to Jarl Olav with news from Nifelheim.

"By Thor's belly button!" Trolgar snarls as he tries to get back on his feet after the crash. "What are you up to?"

"I'm sorry, but aren't you the leader of the gray gnomes?" asks the servant eagerly.

At first Trolgar looks very surprised, then he reaches up, smooths the tufts of hair on his head, and says, "Yes, of course I am the leader of the gray gnomes."

Botvid looks at him in surprise and then snorts, "You, leader! Ha, that's the stupidest thing I've ever heard! We don't have a leader. Gray gnomes don't need a leader."

The servant looks from one gray gnome to the other and doesn't know what to believe.

"Well, silly, today I'm a leader," says Trolgar. "Take me to Jarl Olav at once."

Then Botvid understands and smiles slyly. Trolgar can pretend to be the "leader" if it will bring them some gold. They follow the servant into the great hall but are surprised to see that it isn't Jarl Olav sitting on the throne. Jarl Olav sits on a small, pitiful stool at the side, looking ill. On the throne sits an old man with a long white beard and hair, looking sternly at the two gray gnomes. They feel themselves slowly sinking to the floor in a bow without really intending to do so.

"What can we do for the gentleman?" asks Trolgar, not daring to look at Birk.

"You will leave for the town of North Island at once. You will not rest until you are in the town. There you will find the girl Tora. Take her ellacross and bring it to me as quickly as you can. Do you understand?" Birk's voice booms between the walls, and the gray gnomes feel themselves becoming more and more frightened.

"Of course, the ellacross is coming here," stutters Trolgar. "But what about Tora?"

"Kill her!" Birk roars. "Kill her!"

The gray gnomes nod that they have understood and crawl backwards out of the hall. Once out, they stand up and look at each other in fright. Then they run south as fast as they can, towards the town of North Island … and Tora.

Up in the rafters, Tailtip has heard it all. He hurries off towards the castle courtyard. Out in the yard, he looks around and soon sees the one he's looking for. Up in a small tree sits the magpie Siv who is an old friend of Tailtip's. He quickly climbs up the tree and out onto the branch where Siv is sitting enjoying the sun.

"Hello to you," Siv the magpie crows happily. "You seem to be in a hurry."

"Yes, my fur is on fire!" Tailtip says out of breath. "You must fly to Sigrid at once and tell her that the mysterious man in the castle has sent gray gnomes to the town of North Island. The gray gnomes have order to kill Tora. They know where she is!"

Siv, startled, looks at Tailtip and then takes off towards New Fala village and Sigrid without wasting any time. Tailtip remains in the tree for a while, worried about Tora and Wolf. *Gray gnomes are not to be trifled with. If they are also enchanted by a mysterious man—!* He'd better get back to the great hall quickly and see if he can find out anything more.

With horror, Brage realizes that he is looking at Birk Witchmaster, the mighty wizard of black magic. The man about whom many stories are whispered. His evil, his skill, his cunning. *Maybe I can benefit from this.*

"Go down to your room and get what's on this list. Bring it all here at once!"

Birk hands Brage a dirty old piece of paper on which a list is written in an ancient language. Brage looks at the list and tries to read the first word silently to himself.

"I guess you can't read ancient languages," Birk chuckles. "How can you call yourself a magician?"

Birk makes the magic gesture, and gold dust enters Brage's nose. Brage flinches and then looks at the list again. Now he can read what it says.

"Four rat-tails, a pig's snout, two eagle eggs, a pinch of dragon ash, and a cinnamon stick," Brage reads aloud. "Cinnamon stick?"

"Just because it smells so good. Bring these things to me right away," Birk says imperiously.

"Right away, sir."

Brage bows deeply and backs out of the room, list in hand. He rushes down to his room and immediately starts picking out all the things Birk wants. He knows what the old man is going to cook up. A troll shot! The only question is who will be hit by the troll shot. A strong troll shot can make a person or an animal very ill, or even kill the one who is hit.

Brage really doesn't want to help concoct a troll shot, but he can't resist Birk's wizardry. He collects everything on the list and carries it up to the great hall, where a cauldron of water is already hanging over the crackling fire. He hands the items to Birk and retreats to the door, but Birk narrows his eyes at him and commands,

"Stop! Stay in case I need anything else."

Brage curls up on a chair in a dark corner of the room, hoping the man will forget he's there. Birk starts muttering a gealdor to himself, louder and louder as the smoke comes out of the pot more and more violently. Darkness slowly fills the room; the perpetuating candles go out and finally the only light comes from the fire. The pot sparks and crackles, and a foul smell of sulphur the cinnamon can't mask spreads through every corner of the castle, until the whole castle is wrapped in a dark blanket of smoke and silence.

The people of Silje town stop and look up at the castle, which almost disappears in the black smoke. Everything goes silent. Then comes a very strong flash of lightning followed by a huge *BOOM!*

Inside the great hall, the bang is so loud that it blows Brage and Jarl Olav across the room. They curl up on the floor, their ears ringing. Birk stands unmoved by the fire, looking contentedly into the pot.

Birk takes a wooden spoon and scrapes the mass at the bottom of the pot into a small wooden bowl. He closes the wooden box and places it on the table. After a short while, the box begins to smoke, and runes are burned into the lid without anyone touching it. Then the smoke stops, and the room slowly gets lighter again. Birk looks at the wooden box on the table with satisfaction, then takes a piece of cloth from his coat pocket and wraps it around the box.

Birk looks around and sees Brage sitting on the floor, clutching his ears. "You!" he says, "Take the wooden box to Viva in her cottage in the clearing. Tell her it's a present from Egil the Dwarf King and then leave."

"Why?" Brage now understands who is going to suffer from the troll shot, and he wants no part of this. Brage has always envied Viva's power, but she was once very kind to him, and he doesn't want to hurt her.

"You dare question me? Take the box to Viva immediately!" Birk makes the magic gesture, flinging the gold dust into Brage's nose even though the magician tries to hold his breath. Brage simply must do as Birk says. He picks up the wooden box wrapped in the piece of cloth and sets off for the little cottage in the Ancient Forest. Birk looks after him, satisfied with the day's work.

Still perched on his rafter, Tailtip, shaken and almost deaf from the heavy impact, has watched the runes burn into the wooden box and understands that there is strong dark magic at work. Tailtip couldn't read the runes but tries to remember them so he can scratch them out to show Sigrid. Then he dashes off to look for a lift to New Fala village.

17

Gray Gnomes on the Hunt

As the ferry docks for the last time that evening, two passengers disembark and walk towards the square. They wear cloaks with hoods covering their faces and limp as they walk. They walk out into the square and stand looking in all directions. They sniff the air with their big noses and giggle when they smell to the north.

"Do you think it smells like wolf that way?" asks the tallest.

"Yes, wolves and scabby ravens," the other sniggers. "Shall we see if we've found Tora?"

The two gray gnomes Trolgar and Botvid wrap their cloaks tighter around their gnarled bodies so they won't be recognized, as gray gnomes are not welcome in the town of North Island. They walk towards the north end of the square and stop when they see a sign on a shop:

MEDICINES BY

TRULS AND TORE

Inside the shop, they see an elderly man and a boy putting bottles and cans on the shelves. There are no customers in the shop but there are plenty of people in the square. The gray gnomes sniff the air for Tora's scent. Then they spot Wolf inside the shop and look at each other with satisfaction.

"Look at that!" says Botvid, pleased. "A scabby wolf and a boy."

"She can cut her hair as short as she likes, but we know who she is," says Trolgar quietly. "Now we just must wait for them to fall asleep. Then we can sneak in and get that ellacross that everyone's crazy about."

"We must kill Wolf first," sighs Botvid, scratching his face. "He'll tear us to pieces otherwise."

"Yes, we won't get a moment's peace if the wolf survives but not Tora. You know what Birk ordered. Not that we like it, but we have no choice." Trolgar sighs and looks genuinely sad. Gray gnomes do not like to kill unless they are in real danger. They can steal, kidnap, lie, deceive, and fight but never kill just because another person tells them to, but this time they can't resist Birk's magic powder.

"We'll have to find something we can kill them with," says Botvid quietly. "You watch outside the shop, and I'll go and find us a couple of weapons."

Botvid sneaks away along the houses and disappears among the people in the square. Trolgar pulls his coat around him, adjusts his hood so that it safely hides his face, and stands guard.

It takes a long time before Botvid returns empty-handed. "I can't find anything we can hit them with. This must be the cleanest city there is," sighs the gray gnome.

"Strange," says Trolgar. "There's always old stuff lying around somewhere. Well, we'll just have to surprise them when they're asleep."

The gray gnomes wrap their coats around them and begin their long wait for the town to fall asleep.

The town grows quieter as night descends upon it. After a couple of hours, the square is mostly empty, and Tora turns off the lights in the shop. The two gray gnomes wait for half an hour, then they begin to walk along the walls of the houses towards the shop. In the dark shadows behind them, they don't see a sword glint once in the torchlight before all is dark again. The gray gnomes stop at the door of the shop.

"If you go over to Wolf and hit him really hard with a chair, I'll take the old man," whispers Trolgar.

"Okay, but you must promise to help me with the wolf if I miss," whispers Botvid nervously.

"Sure," says Trolgar, but he's not really going to do it. If they don't kill the wolf on the first hit, they'll have to run as fast as they can.

The gray gnomes slowly and quietly open the door to the shop. They stand still and listen for a long moment. The only sounds are loud snores from a room further in. They can glimpse Wolf curled up under a blanket next to the hearth, but the fire has gone out and the room is very dark.

Botvid grabs a stool and walks towards the sleeping wolf. Trolgar sneaks quietly further into the shop, past the big bench with all the glass bottles and jars, towards the back room where you can hear someone snoring loudly.

Botvid raises the stool high above his head, then he slams it as hard as he can straight down on the curled-up wolf.

BOOM!

As the stool hits the blanket, a bright flash lights up the room, and a boom echoes through the shop. Botvid is so frightened that he falls over, deafened by the impact.

Meanwhile outside in the square, black shadows have sneaked up to the shop. Ten guards who have followed the gray gnomes under cover of darkness, now rush into the store and quickly tie up the confused Botvid who has dropped to the floor. Four guards lift the gray gnome now tied with rope and carry him out from the shop.

In the back room, other strong men from the local police pounce on Trolgar and tie him up before he can react. They lift Trolgar over their heads and carry him out into the square. Once both gray gnomes are captured, Tora, Truls and Wolf enter the shop again from the square.

"Wow, what a bang," says the watch commander to Truls. They stand looking at the black soot stain and the smoking grey blanket on the floor in front of the fireplace.

"Yes, it's an invention that comes from China," Truls says. "It's called gunpowder. All it takes is a little powder to make it go off really loud."

Wolf snorts repeatedly. The faint stench that fills the room irritates his sensitive nose. "Not only do gray gnomes stink on their own, but your ellacross makes them stink even from a distance," snorts the wolf.

"Yes, that spell you have on the ellacross is really effective," says Truls. "It started to smell as soon as the gray gnomes got off the ferry."

"Well, our plan worked." The watch commander nods pleased. "You simply walked straight through the house and out to safety in the alley behind. Meanwhile, some of my guards sneaked in and waited for the gray gnomes inside Truls' room."

"Yes, and it was a nice touch that one of the guards was instructed to snore loudly when the door to the shop opened," Tora laughs. "What's happening to the gray gnomes now?" Tora wonders.

"There is a ship down in the harbour that will sail south tomorrow. They're taking the gray gnomes and dropping them far from here," says the watch commander.

"Sounds good," says Truls with a sigh. "Thanks for your help tonight!"

"Only good if we can help each other. After all, it's us townspeople who should be thanking you two for all the help we get from your medicines and divinations," says the watch commander, gesturing for the remaining guards to go outside. "Good night!"

"Good night," says Truls. "Let's go to bed!"

Truls and Tora go into their rooms, and Wolf stands guard at the shop door. You never know what will happen on a dark night.

18

Troll Snot and Black Magic

B rage stands in the clearing in the Ancient Forest and looks at Viva's cottage. The air is filled with the scent of flowers and the chirping of all the small birds chattering pleasantly in the trees and bushes. The clearing is quiet and pleasant, and Brage suddenly feels calm and pleased with himself. The door to the cottage opens, and Viva steps out onto the grass.

"Welcome, Brage," she calls to the man who is hesitating a little way away. "Come into the cottage for a moment and we'll talk."

"Thank you," says Brage hesitantly, unsure of how to behave.

He walks over to the cottage and through the low door. He wonders how the blind Viva knew he was standing there, and suddenly becomes very worried when he sees two white elves sitting at the table inside the cottage. It is the first time Brage has seen a white elf. He is amazed by their beauty, their long silver-white hair, their ice-blue eyes, and their radiant smiles. The patterns of the white suits in silver threads move and change shape all the time, like a gentle dance.

"Please sit down, Brage," says Viva, pulling out a chair. "Nice of you to visit. This are my friends Pail and Silver."

"Thank you," says Brage nervously, bows towards the elves and sits down.

The white elves' ice-blue eyes look at him kindly, but it feels like they can see right through him and know why he's here. Viva sets out some food and drink and then sits down at the table.

"How are things at the castle? Have you got rid of all the manure?" she asks, and the three of them smile happily at the memory.

"Yes, yes, it's gone," Brage says, twisting in his chair. "It was a funny idea." He tries to laugh a little, but it sounds strange, so he stops immediately.

"So, what can I help you with today? You must want something special, because you've never visited me before," says Viva.

"I've brought you a box from the lord of the castle," says Brage, rummaging through his large pockets for the wooden box.

"Oh, Jarl Olav has sent you here with a gift. Well, well, well!" Viva laughs.

The white elves sit quietly and watch Brage, who is getting more and more nervous. He is convinced the white elves know what he is thinking.

"No, not Jarl Olav. Mr Birk runs the castle now," Brage explains.

"So, Birk Witchmaster is back in Nordanland," says Viva thoughtfully. "That explains a lot. I thought he was wise enough to stay away from here. The last time he was here, Queen Ella sent him away in the clutches of a big dragon called Nidhugg."

"Dragon? There are no dragons, are there?" Brage snorts nervously. "It's just something you say to scare the kids to bed at night."

"Yes, there are dragons, but unfortunately not as many as there were hundreds of years ago," says Viva, smiling. "Nidhugg is a nice guy, as long as you're friendly."

"Well, I don't have time to sit here and listen to children's stories," Brage says irritably. He puts the wooden box wrapped in cloth on the table. "Here's the present from Mr Birk. I think you'd better open it right away." Brage pushes the wooden box towards Viva.

You should go now. Go south until you reach a big city and stay there. Brage looks around in confusion at what he has heard. No one around the table has said anything. He frowns. The voice repeats itself, and this time he knows it's inside his head.

19

Page 23

Sigrid walks through the forest towards Nifelheim as the sun slowly sinks behind the trees. The moon hangs just above the spruce peaks, almost full and faintly red. She doesn't have long to prepare for the blood moon. One thing she knows for certain is that Birk Witchmaster will be prepared. He's had time to devise a cunning revenge in all his years in exile.

Birk has already tried to kill Viva twice in a short time. First, he cast a draug sleep curse, and then he sent a troll shot. A troll shot! Now he's gone too far. Sigrid will do everything she can to put an end to the witchmaster once and for all.

Sigrid enters the great hall of Nifelheim. Egil the Dwarf King and Grim Dwarf are sitting by the fire, drinking mead and talking. It's such a peaceful scene that it's hard to believe that the dwarfs could be ready for battle in minutes. Sigrid pulls out a chair and sinks into the warmth of the fire with a sigh.

"Good evening, Sigrid," the dwarfs greet her.

"You look worried," says Egil. "Has something happened?"

"Birk is back and has taken over Silje Castle," Sigrid says tired and worried. "Jarl Olav is under a gealdor and Brage is heading south, away from Nordanland and Birk."

"Birk!" Grim exclaims. "That cunning and dangerous witch!"

"Today he sent a troll shot to Viva." Sigrid's voice trembles with anger. "Luckily it didn't work."

"But what has happened to our friend the dragon Nidhugg? I thought he was keeping an eye on him," says Egil.

"I don't know," says Sigrid. "I'll ask the black elves to try and find out. Maybe Nidhugg is sick and needs help. In the meantime, we must get ready for the blood moon and whatever Birk can come up with. Gray gnomes, glutton hogs, oknytt, and trolls have all been seen on the edges of the forest. Something is going on."

"We can ask some elves to go to the edges of the forest to keep an extra watch," suggests Grim. "I can go with Atte Black Elf to the northern part. We'll leave early tomorrow morning."

Grim gets up, says goodbye, and goes to find his friend Atte Black Elf so they can pack for their scouting trip. Sigrid and Egil sit and plan for a few more hours before they go to bed. The days ahead are going to be long and hard.

In the north, just where the Ancient Forest begins, some elves are already perched on top of a thousand-year-old spruce tree, peering into the mountains. Elves can see further and hear better than humans, so they make excellent scouts. They see faraway smoke from hundreds of campfires curling up into the evening sky. In recent days, trolls, gray gnomes, oknytt, even some mountain giants have gathered in the valley around the lake called Mimer's Well. The camp is filling up with more creatures all the time.

The elves write a message on a small piece of paper and tie it around the leg of a pigeon. Then they politely ask the pigeon to fly quickly to Nifelheim and deliver the message to Egil or Sigrid. They must gather the army and get ready to defend Nordanland.

In the town of North Island, Tora can't sleep. She has been tossing and turning in bed for quite a while, restless and anxious. Then she suddenly remembers the book that Viva wanted her to read that last day in the cottage. After the old man in disguise arrived and she had to leave quickly, she had just put the book in her bag without thinking about it since. Tora rummages the book out of her bag and goes out of her room, into the shop.

Stomp Mush and Glutton Sausage

The recipe is adapted to our time for serving two people.

Ingredients

4–6 potatoes, preferably the floury kind, about 0,5 kilograms

2–4 carrots, depending on size

4 – 6 pork or turkey sausage or similar, about 400-500 grams

1 yellow onion

oil for pan-frying

2–4 tablespoons mustard, preferably coarsely ground, divided

3 decilitres cream

salt to taste

a knob of butter

Peel the carrots and potatoes. Cut carrots into "coins" and divide the potatoes into four halves. Put the carrot and potato pieces in a pot and add water to cover. Boil until soft, about 20 minutes.

Meanwhile, peel and chop the onions. Cut the sausage into four pieces each.

Pour some oil into a frying pan. When it is hot, add the chopped onion. Let fry for about a minute, stirring occasionally.

Add the sausage pieces to the onion. Continue to fry until they are nicely browned and cooked through. Stir occasionally!

Add 2 tablespoons of the mustard to the sausage-onion mixture, then pour in the cream. Stir to distribute. Add more mustard or salt to taste.

When the sausage mixture is heated through, remove and set aside to keep warm.

When the potatoes and carrots are soft, drain and return them to the pot. Take a potato masher and mash them coarsely. There should be chunks left in the mash.

Add a knob of butter and season to taste. Add salt if necessary.

Divide the vegetable mush between two plates and serve the sausage mixture on top.

Enjoy your meal!

Words to Know

beacon   fires lit on high ground so they can be seen from far away to warn people

bid roll   a message passed on in a form of a relay

black elf   a tall, slender people who have long black hair and often wear black clothes

draug   an evil spirit, the living dead

dwarf   a short, strong, helpful, friendly people

ellacross   a cross with a circle in it; the wearer is protected by Odin and/or a spell

flatfoot   a people who are short and strong, with big ears and black hair, and who live in Lawland and are good at keeping order

gealdor   spell

giant   a big, strong, helpful people

glutton hog   a species of very large boar with bristly hair on its back, known for its ill temper

gray gnomes   a short, mean, cunning people with strong muscles and a bony face with a big nose

mastodon   large elephant with furry coat and huge tusks

mountain giant a race of mountain-dwelling giants who are very big, strong, and always angry with humans and dwarfs

moon-turn   month

Nix	a naked man who lives by the water and plays the violin so that people are attracted to the water by the music
oknytt	small, yellowish, mean creatures with long, floppy ears
pixies	a short, easily angered people who wear clothes that make them invisible in the wild
runes	letters carved into wood or stone, can be magical
seid	healer, magician; cures and helps the sick, can see into the future, can speak different languages and sometimes even with animals.
sorcerer	male magician with evil intentions
sun-turn	year
ting	a council where leaders gather to decide important things such as going to war
troll shot	a special spell that makes you sick or kills you
white elf	a very tall, slender people with long silver-white hair, often wearing white clothes

Printed in the United States
by Baker & Taylor Publisher Services